The Ace of Spades
What if one card changed your life?

Venkat Raman V

Ukiyoto Publishing

All global publishing rights are held by

Ukiyoto Publishing

Published in 2024

Content Copyright © Venkat Raman V

ISBN 9789364949606

*All rights reserved.
No part of this publication may be reproduced,
transmitted, or stored in a retrieval system, in any form
by any means, electronic, mechanical, photocopying,
recording or otherwise, without the prior permission of
the publisher.*

The moral rights of the authors have been asserted.

*This is a work of fiction. Names, characters, businesses,
places, events, locales, and incidents are either the
products of the author's imagination or used in a
fictitious manner. Any resemblance to actual persons,
living or dead, or actual events is purely coincidental.*

*This book is sold subject to the condition that it shall not by
way of trade or otherwise, be lent, resold, hired out or
otherwise circulated, without the publisher's prior
consent, in any form of binding or cover other than that in
which it is published.*

www.ukiyoto.com

Dedicated to my father who encourages my writing aspirations and to all my friends who have been enthusiastic critics

What if one card changed everything?

Cards come in man's life at many a time. Cards make luck, they help a man pass time, they can be an identity or in some cases, they can simply mean death. Not getting into any of those, cards are most widely used as a means to play a game. A game so popular and hand-in-hand with betting. So widely played, millions are made and billions are lost to it. A card can have a great impact on someone, whether it makes him money or it means something more.

Gavin Hale lay on his bed with his girlfriend Trudy lying over him. It was past noon but he lay relaxed. They had only slept at dawn. Gavin was a programmer by profession. He only worked freelance. He was good at what he did and he earned more than he could ever dream of spending. That helped him spend his time as he pleased. Trudy was fun but sensible. She took care of him and she was cute. Trudy was the kind of girl one would want to be with for life.

"It's late, my darling" he said as she snuggled sleepily.

"It's not like you have work to do," she said with her eyes closed.

"I promised Nellie that I'd take her to the museum today," he said.

Connelly was his sister's seven-year-old daughter. His sister Rebecca was a single mother. She took care of his parents and stayed in his hometown. Connelly stayed in one of the best boarding schools in the country thanks to Gavin. It was in the same city as his and he offered to get her into the school. Gavin visited her often. It was one of his most favourite things to do. She was sweet and she loved the company of her uncle.

He would usually bring her home and they'd spend time with Trudy, eating pizza and watching her favourite shows on TV. Occasionally, Trudy would cook something special for them. However, this week she wanted to go to the museum. A new exhibit dedicated to cartoons was about to open. It was not very big but Connelly loved cartoons and she wanted to see this one badly.

"Sure, say 'hi' to her for me" said Trudy as she rolled away.

Gavin got up and began to freshen up. He was supposed to meet her by four in the evening and he had never been late yet. He made himself look presentable.

"Hi, Uncle Gav" she said in a shrill, happy voice as she ran towards him. He hoisted her into the air and caught her, amused by the sound of her giggling.

"Have a good time with her Mr. Hale ….," began the hostel warden.

" …. and I'll have her back in time. Pleasure meeting you, Mr. Warden" he said as he began to listen to his niece talk animatedly about all that happened since his last visit.

He placed her on his shoulders as they left the school compound.

"Where are we off to, Uncle Gav?" she asked.

"To the museum like you wanted to sweetheart," he answered as he moved forward.

Nellie's happiness was short lived as they saw the notice in front of the museum that read, 'EXHIBIT ON CARTOONS POSTPONED UNTIL FURTHER NOTICE. WE REGRET THE INCONVENIENCE CAUSED'

"Let's go back, Uncle Gav" she said looking crestfallen.

"Come on! Let's go into the museum," he said trying to cheer her up.

"I'm seven, uncle Gav. I know what the museum has. Without the cartoons, it's a boring place" she said.

"Come on Nellie. It's not bad. You haven't been to the museum with me, have you?" he asked cheerfully.

"What's so special about going in with you?" asked Nellie sharply.

"Well …," began Gavin with no idea what he was going to say, "I explain stuff funny"

"Yeah. Funny man!" she said grumpily.

"Come on," said Gavin softly.

Nellie followed him reluctantly. Gavin tried hard to be funny as he showed Nellie around the museum. Gavin was a natural at being funny but being funny at a museum was difficult even for him. Nellie did enjoy herself, giggling at what Gavin had to say but Gavin had used up all his lines in a matter of minutes.

"This place is boring," said Nellie as they came in front of an exhibit that was a statue of a grumpy man labeled, 'King Francis – The ace of spades'

"Okay," began Gavin almost giving up, "I guess I'll just have to punch this …. King Francis and take you to dinner," she said.

"Sounds good but you can't punch him," said Nellie.

"I can too," said Gavin.

"It says here that King Francis was a sadist who was murdered by his own people and that he vowed to take vengeance on the world. His spirit lies within this statue," said Nellie reading the inscription.

"So?" asked Gavin.

"Come on uncle Gav. We know that you are the chicken in the family. Aunt Trudy has to kill spiders for you. Are you really going to punch a cursed statue?" asked Nellie mockingly.

"I am not a chicken," said Gavin defensively.

"You don't need to defend yourself uncle Gav. I love you no matter what," she said noticing the change in Gavin's tone.

Gavin read the inscription, "Statue found in the palace of King Francis".

Gavin had read about this guy. He was the one who used the Ace of Spades as his signature in his kills. Gavin waited for a moment and then spoke, "What if I punch this thing? Will you agree that I am not a chicken?".

"You don't need to do that," began Nellie but Gavin jumped over the small fence and rushed to the statue. His heart began to beat faster in fear. He quickly jabbed the statue, turned his back to Nellie and whispered in fear, "Don't kill me," and walked back to Nellie, grinning widely.

"What do you say now?" he asked her triumphantly.

"You are such a baby," she said with a smile.

"I see that you are enjoying the King Francis exhibit," said a guide who walked towards them.

"You could say that," said Nellie sarcastically.

"This is a very powerful piece you know. Everything but this was destroyed in his palace. Makes you wonder, doesn't it?" he said looking at the statue.

"That's an ugly piece of work," said Gavin mockingly.

"King Francis was a great ruler. Terrible but great. He was a great patron of the arts, a scholar and a great warrior. Some say he went mad," said the guide.

"Hmmm," said Gavin looking at the statue.

"Do you know why this statue was not destroyed?" he asked softly.

"Like I said, it is an ugly piece of work," said Gavin mockingly.

"King Francis loved this statue. It is believed that his spirit lives in it. The last man who attempted to destroy it killed himself," said the guide.

Gavin swallowed nervously but did his best to conceal his fear. He had a lively dinner with Nellie at the 'Best Burgers' outlet nearby and dropped her back at school.

That night, he sat on his bed, playing a game on his PlayStation. His TV on the wall was one of his prized possessions. He had got it from Howard Stringer as a gift for one of the programs that he wrote for a television model. He wore headphones to keep the sound to himself. Trudy sat beside him, looking into their finances. She wore her specs on the tip of her nose. The glass was more of an accessory.

"How was your day with Nellie?" she asked as Gavin removed the headset and settled down.

He took a deep breath and leaned on her. "It was fine but she called me a coward," said Gavin.

"A coward?" asked Trudy in surprise. She had stopped jabbing her calculator.

"Not by the exact word but she called me the chicken of the family," he said.

"Oh!" said Trudy, chuckled and returned to working on her calculator.

"You think so too?" he asked surprised by her silence.

"You are not a coward Gavin but you are afraid of a lot of things," she said not looking at him.

"I am not," he retorted.

"You are and you know it. Let's face it. I have to kill spiders for you. You are a sweet guy. Probably the sweetest guy I have and will ever meet but you scare easy," she said.

"I don't!" he said defensively.

"You asked me to move in with you because you were afraid to live alone," she said.

"Why did you move in then?" asked Gavin moving to have a good look at her face.

"You love me," she said sharply.

"Oh …. And you?" he asked.

"Do you even need to ask me that?" she said turning to him.

"I know I don't need to know. You are my life now but I want you to know that you can count on me when you need me. I won't be scared or anything," he said seriously.

Trudy stopped working and placed a hand on his cheek. She looked at him fondly. She pulled him closer and gave him a kiss on his cheek. "Right!" she said turned away grinning.

Gavin walked along the museum corridor alone. His heart was beating faster than ever. He walked cautiously to the exhibit of King Francis. He looked for the statue but it was gone.

As he looked around, he felt a cold stony touch on his shoulder. He slowly turned with his heart rattling on his ribs to face the statue of King Francis himself.

"Hello," growled the statue.

Gavin tumbled and fell backwards. He tried to crawl away in fear.

"Are you afraid now, little one?" the statue growled but this time, Gavin was being taunted.

"I never meant to offend you," he began nervously.

"That's what you all say, insolent creatures! You people never learnt your place. You do not know how to respect a King," he roared.

"Don't do anything to me. I am sorry," pleaded Gavin.

"You are not sorry," he sniped. "But you will be," he said menacingly and roared.

Gavin jolted awake in his bed. It took a few minutes for him to realize that it was just a dream. He lay awake, staring blankly at the ceiling. As he turned, he saw that Trudy had fallen asleep too. She had rolled away and was close to falling off the bed. He quickly pulled her close and adjusted her blankets.

When he got up and went to wash his face, it was almost dawn. He felt fresh as he repeatedly splashed his face with water. As he dried his face with a towel, he saw a card lying on the ground. It was strange as nothing was ever out of place in his apartment. As he bent down to look at it, he realized that it was the Ace of Spades.

He did not remember when he last played cards. It had been a year and a half since he played poker. He picked up the card to place it with the pack. Just as he was about to place it, he turned the card.

He wondered for a moment if it was a joke. On the back of the card was a picture of his mother. It was weird. He did not know how the picture got there. He put it in his pocket. Just as he kept pondering over it, his phone rang loudly. Trudy woke up and took the call sleepily. She immediately froze. Her face became white.

"What?" asked Gavin.

She raised her hand to stop him. She spoke for a minute and ended the call with a deep breath.

"Sit down honey. There's something that I have to tell you," she said looking serious.

As he sat next to her, she held his hands. Her eyes had become watery but her voice was steady.

"What is it?" he asked her.

"Honey, I just received news that your mother passed away an hour ago," she said in a sad voice. Her tone was low and her voice was pacifying but it did nothing to stop the tears that began to flow down his cheeks. Gavin put his head on his knees and lost track of things.

In about an hour, they were in their car. Trudy drove as Gavin lay curled up in the back seat. He stared blankly at the roof of the car as it moved swiftly. Trudy knew that he did not want to talk. She played music as the car moved. Not struck as deeply by the fact as Gavin, Nellie sat quietly in the passenger seat.

Gavin checked his pocket to look for the card with his mother's picture but it was missing. He slowly drifted off to sleep.

When he reached his house, it was different. His house was gloomy. He had always come home only on happy occasions. This was a first. He saw his father sitting across the room, eyes closed and tears flowing from his eyes. His sister walked slowly to hug Nellie. Nellie remained indifferent to all that was happening around her but she acted like she understood the situation.

"Where is she?" asked Trudy.

"At the funeral home," said Rebecca.

"How did it happen?" asked Gavin, speaking for the first time in hours. He was thankful to Trudy for taking over for him during the travel and in making arrangements. He sat next to his father, holding his hand.

"She slept and never quite got up," said Rebecca coming over and sitting next to him.

"Was she sick or anything?" asked Gavin.

"She was fine. She wanted to cook something special yesterday after a long time. She made lasagna," said

Rebecca. "She was talking about you as we had dinner. You always loved her lasagna," she said fondly.

Gavin couldn't help but remember flashes of his childhood. His mother had been a wonderful cook and if it weren't for a very fast rate of metabolism, he'd have grown up to be a very fat kid.

Gavin slowly walked to the kitchen. He could still smell the lasagna. The twenty-year-old lasagna tray lay in the sink but the room still had the aroma. As he closed his eyes, he could feel his mother's presence.

"She kept some in the fridge and she got reminded of you," said Rebecca.

In a few minutes, Gavin sat in front of the heated lasagna. He could not get himself to believe that this would be the last time that he would taste his mother's cooking. He slowly began to eat. Just as he licked the plate clean, he saw something on the ground.

It was an Ace of Spades card on the floor. He picked it up. He hesitated for a moment and then turned it. It was not his mother's picture but a picture of Jim Colt, his best friend and his accountant. It looked weird for a moment but his mind raced back to memories of his mother.

They got dressed up and left for the funeral home. Gavin let his tears flow freely as he stood next to the casket. His mother looked peaceful. It was as though she was sleeping. As Gavin looked closer, he could see a card placed carefully on the top of the casket.

Gavin hesitated and then picked it up. It was an Ace of Spades. He turned the card to see a picture of his mother. It was the same that he had seen before. As he stared at it, letters appeared in gold on the card.

'AND SO, IT BEGINS …'

Gavin dropped the card and stepped back in surprise.

"Gav? What happened?" came Trudy's voice.

Gavin looked up to see Trudy walking towards him. He looked down again but the card was gone. Gavin looked up again, puzzled by what had happened.

"Something wrong honey?" she asked looking concerned.

"No. Just a little dizzy," said Gavin.

Gavin stayed in the shadows for the entire duration of the funeral. His feelings of grief, coupled with the confusion caused by the cards made him want to be alone. Trudy was doing his job of being the host, shooting anxious glances at him from time to time. He tried to smile reassuringly but he was never good in hiding his feelings.

"Something's wrong with you, Gavin" said Trudy as they drove back from the funeral home.

"Nothing. I'm sad," said Gavin defensively.

"No. I would have understood that. You looked confused and afraid. What is the matter? Is something wrong?" she asked softly.

"Nothing. I just can't believe that she's gone already," said Gavin.

"I know, honey. I know how hard it must be on you," she said placing a hand gently on his shoulder.

Gavin closed his eyes as she drove them home. Gavin did not feel like leaving his mom's house. They decided to stay there for a while. Gavin could work from anywhere and Trudy called her workplace to arrange to work remotely.

It was five days after the funeral when Jim Colt called Gavin.

"Hey Gav," he said.

"Hello, Jim" replied Gavin.

"When are you getting back Gav?" he asked.

"Not anytime soon," said Gavin.

"I need you to sign a couple of documents for me, Gav" he said.

"Couldn't I fax it over?" asked Gavin.

"Not possible. The pay is a hundred grand. I don't want any hic-cups. You can take the next flight out," he said dismissively.

"Why don't you come here?" asked Gavin.

"I don't know Gav …," began Jim.

"Come on. You'll have fun. Take the next flight. It will hardly take you two hours to reach here," said Gavin.

"Alright. I'll be there tomorrow," said Jim with a sigh.

Gavin heaved a sigh of relief as Trudy stroked his hair. He lay on her lap silently in his study. He did not want to leave his mother's house. Not anytime soon. Things had happened so quickly.

Trudy gently kissed him on his forehead. He slowly dozed off and was woken up. It was morning when he came back to his senses.

"Gav, we have to go. Pull on some clothes," said Trudy. There was an anxious look on her face.

"What's the matter, honey?" asked Gavin.

"Get in the car. I'll tell you on the way," said Trudy.

Gavin got ready quickly and got into the car. "What happened?" he asked as the car began to move.

"I got a call from the highway patrol. Jim met with an accident when he was driving here," she said holding back tears.

"What?" asked Gavin in surprise.

"He couldn't get a flight. He called me to tell me that he was driving here," she said.

Jim was Gavin's best friend. He couldn't help but feel anxious. "Where is he now?" asked Gavin.

"They've told me to get to the hospital immediately," she said. Her voice seemed to falter.

Gavin remained silent the whole way. Trudy enquired at the hospital reception and took him to the emergency ward. She spoke to someone who looked like a doctor. With tears in her eyes, she came back to him and hugged him. That told Gavin all that he needed to know. Gavin broke down. It took him about ten minutes to pull himself back together. Two of his most favourite people had met tragic ends in such short intervals.

He was allowed to go and look at Jim's body before they took it to the morgue. He walked alone into the room. Jim was covered till the neck with white cloth. His face was plain except for a wound on his forehead which had now been cleaned.

The Ace of Spades

As Gavin stood in silence, he noticed a card on the chest of Jim. It was an Ace of Spades. Heart pounding, Gavin picked up the card and turned it. The card had a picture of his father. Gold letters appeared on the card as Gavin held it. 'YOU KNOW WHAT THIS MEANS'

Gavin stood in shock. Just then, the door opened and Trudy entered. Gavin looked at her and then turned to look at the card in his hand. The card had disappeared. Trudy had not noticed anything. She simply came over to him and hugged him.

Gavin was both depressed and anxious. It was he who had asked Jim to come over. If he had not, Jim would not have met with an accident. It then hit him. He had to get to his dad because he was the next target.

"Stay here Trudy. I need to go check on something," he told her.

"Gavin, do you need to go now?" she asked anxiously.

"Yes, honey. This cannot wait. Give me the keys," he said dismissively.

In a matter of minutes, Gavin was racing back home. He kept calling his dad but he was not answering his phone. After calling him a few more times, he called his sister.

"Hey Gav, how's Jim?" she asked as she answered.

"It doesn't matter. Where's dad?" he asked desperately.

"What's the matter Gavin? You sound anxious," she said sounding concerned.

"There's no time Becky. Just tell me where dad is," he said.

"Is something wrong?" she asked.

"No. Just tell me where dad is," he hissed.

"He's gone to Emery's to buy some groceries," said Rebecca.

Gavin ended the call and began to drive even faster towards the destination. Emery's was a very large store that sold everything from household supplies to food and beverages. As he moved through the aisles, searching frantically for his dad, he noticed it. A wooden crate on one of the top shelves was wobbling and standing right below was his dad.

Adrenaline rushing, Gavin darted and pushed his father out of the way. The crate landed with a loud crash, missing them by inches.

"What happened? How did you get here?" asked his father in surprise.

Gavin was still gasping for breath as he lay flat on the ground next to his dad. People nearby rushed to help them up. Gavin could not help but wonder who or what was trying to kill the people behind the cards.

As he was being helped up, Gavin gazed at the shattered remains of the crate. He could see on the wood, the image of a single black spade.

Gavin could not get himself to talk. His father ended his shopping abruptly under Gavin's insistence and they got back home. Gavin asked Rebecca and his dad to come back with him for a few days. After much persistence, they agreed. Gavin spent the remainder of his stay watching over his dad.

Gavin couldn't help but think about King Francis. The cards had started appearing only after the visit to the museum. Gavin paced nervously as Trudy came to him.

"Something's wrong Gavin," she said, sitting on the couch.

"What honey?" he asked trying to sound normal.

"You've been too anxious all the time, honey. Is there a problem that I need to know about?" she asked.

"Nothing, honey. I'm just a bit pre-occupied," he said dismissively.

"Pre-occupied with what? You just lost two very important people in your life. I can understand if you are grieving but you seem to be tensed," she said.

"It's nothing," he said.

"You can't lie to me Gav. I know you better than anyone else," she said soothingly.

"Let this one go," he said.

"When you want to talk about it …," she began.

"You'll be the first one I come to," he said completing her sentence.

Gavin reached forward and gently kissed her on her forehead. Trudy walked away but Gavin could see that she was anxious too. He did not want to burden her with what was going on. At the least, not until he was sure what it was.

Gavin walked to the door and opened it. However, it was not the familiar hallway that he could see. It was a long room with a lot of pillars and decorations.

Gavin could see that the curtains were made of silk. There were a lot of expensive things in the room. Everything in the room looked like it belonged in a palace. Just as the thought struck Gavin, he heard someone clearing their throat.

"Who are you?" asked Gavin to a man who stood with a crown and a very good-looking fur coat. Inside the fur coat was a magenta dress and a lot of jewelry. The man simply stared at Gavin as he began pacing around. His face was filled with both scorn and disgust. Gavin knew that this was the real King Francis.

As King Francis continued to keep his eye on Gavin as he moved, his face began to show anger.

"What do you want?" asked Gavin nervously.

"You dare speak to me unless spoken to? You imbecile," spat King Francis.

"You brought me here. It's only fair that you tell me why," said Gavin.

"You will be very sorry you insulted me," hissed King Francis.

"Hey look. I did not mean to offend you or anything. I'm sorry if I did something ….," began Gavin nervously.

"You are not sorry," growled King Francis. His eyes were like they were on fire. However, after an angry stare, his lips curved into a smile. "But you will be," he said.

"What do you mean I will be?" asked Gavin angrily. He was getting tired of this person. He had enough on his mind.

King Francis stared angrily at Gavin. "Have you not figured you out yet genius? It was I who killed your mother. It was I who killed Jim Colt and it is your fault entirely," he said sharply.

"You can't be serious," said Gavin in disbelief.

"You saw the cards did you not? Why do you think the Ace of Spades is called the 'death card'? I started the practice and the lore has carried on. Now, I will take away all those you love. You know who's next," said King Francis and began laughing like a maniac.

In a fit of rage, Gavin rushed at King Francis but the King and the room vanished, leaving Gavin to stand in the familiar hallway, clueless with all that had happened.

Gavin drove in the second car with his father. The other drivers on the road seemed particularly insane and twice or thrice, they come to clashing but turned away at the last moment.

Gavin remained silent and let music play as he drove. His father too remained silent as the music brought him memories of his deceased wife.

Gavin kept shooting nervous glances at his father who remained oblivious to all that was around him. Gavin was quite pleased when they got home. Two days passed very slowly. Gavin distracted himself with some work over the next two days in an attempt to take his mind off things. He kept them oblivious to all that he knew.

It was a Sunday when Nellie had to be taken back to school. They all went together to drop her off at school. Trudy drove on their way back home with his father riding shotgun. He had finally smiled that day and Gavin was pleased to let him be.

As they drove home, Gavin lazily stared outside the window. Just as they entered the freeway, Gavin saw a clown car go past them. On the door of the car was a huge sticker of an Ace of Spades. Gavin's heart began to beat faster. Just as he was watching it, the car swerved dangerously. The truck running parallel to it had to immediately switch lanes. The truck collided head on with a bus and one after the other, vehicles crashed and toppled. Trudy screeched the car to an abrupt stop as they watched the catastrophe.

Close to fifty vehicles were involved in the crash. Just as they tried to get out of the car, one of the cars that had toppled exploded. A piece of metal flew towards the car. Just as Gavin watched, the piece of metal broke through the glass and hit his father in the neck, severing his head completely.

Gavin's body froze and when he came back to his senses, both women were screaming at the sight of his decapitated father. Gavin could not find his voice but fear and rage filled him as tears rolled down his cheek. Gavin couldn't remember much of what happened next. All he could remember was flashes of the emergency medical team rushing to them, the ride to the hospital and vague memories.

Gavin woke up from his bed, not knowing how he got there. He did not want to get up. The memories were something that he wanted to lose. However, there was nothing that he could do. After about ten minutes, he forced himself to go and freshen up. Gavin looked at himself on the mirror to see himself looking unshaven and looking like he'd been beaten up badly.

As he entered the dining room, there was a bowl of scrambled eggs. Rebecca sat with her head on the table, her hair covering her face. Trudy sat next to her, staring blankly at the ceiling as she sipped a cup of coffee. Gavin sat on the other side of the table. Trudy turned to him but there was no sign of any greeting. Gavin could smell the aroma of scrambled eggs but nobody felt hungry. Gavin stared around blankly for a while after which he noticed that Trudy was serving breakfast.

He turned to protest but she said calmly, "You can't stay hungry forever"

Reluctantly, Gavin began to eat. In no time, all the plates were empty. As Gavin looked at Rebecca, he noticed her tube top. It had a large image of a Spade. Gavin knew what it meant. As both fear and anger overwhelmed him, tears flowed down his cheek. Not knowing why, Trudy placed a soothing hand on his shoulder.

Gavin had spent a while researching about the card. The Ace of Spades was known as the 'death card'. Though the name came from the game of cards, it was found often in ancient lore. Joe could find nothing about King Francis when he remembered the man from the museum.

Gavin did not waste a second. He was at the museum in the next fifteen minutes. It was almost noon and the place was empty as usual. He kept his eyes open for the guide. As Gavin caught a glimpse of him, the guide was looking towards Gavin in surprise. As he noticed Gavin looking towards him, he grinned.

Gavin took a step forward and the guide took a step backwards. Gavin did not wait. He sprinted towards the guide even before he could think about running, reducing the distance between them in half. The guide ran but he got himself cornered when he went into the men's room.

"What do you want?" he asked nervously.

"Tell me about King Francis," hissed Gavin. He locked the door behind him and firmly stood his ground.

"You can see the exhibit. It has all that you want," said the guide.

"You said something about the statue," hissed Gavin.

"Wait. Is he really hunting you? Is he driving you crazy?" asked the guide. Despite the fear in his face, there was a manic glint in his eye.

"Tell me more about it," growled Gavin.

"The last man who tried to destroy the statue killed himself. Judging by the way you look, you are not far from it," said the guide. He was now totally relaxed.

"I did not try to destroy the statue," said Gavin.

"You must have offended the king," said the guide.

"How do I stop him?" asked Gavin.

"What is he doing to you?" asked the guide.

"He's killing people. People I know," said Gavin.

"Serves you right," spat the guide.

"Excuse me," said Gavin in surprise.

"You heard me," he said mockingly.

"I'm at the end of my line here. Tell me how I stop all this," said Gavin.

"You talk big," he mocked again.

"He's killing my family one by one," said Gavin.

"He will never stop. King Francis will have his revenge," said the guide.

"There is always a way," hissed Gavin.

"I wouldn't tell you now, would I?" he said and began cackling madly.

Gavin begged the guide to help him out but he would not stop laughing. They reached a point when Gavin punched him on the face. He attempted to retaliate but Gavin caught him by the collar and smashed his head on a urinal, breaking it and knocking him out.

***

"Assault and battery? What the hell is wrong with you Gavin?" hissed Trudy as she bailed him out. Gavin had been arrested for attacking the guide. Gavin remained silent as he followed her.

"I've never seen you get into a fight before. What happened to you Gav?" she asked sounding concerned. Gavin noticed her smile faintly and said, "I never knew you could fight". Gavin remained silent. He couldn't reciprocate Trudy's smile.

"Is something wrong honey?" she asked sounding concerned.

Gavin did not know what to tell her. He simply hugged her and whispered, "I'm sorry but I don't know what to say to you".

"What's wrong Gav?" she asked as she patted him gently.

"I don't know Trudy but I can't tell you either. Are you alright with that?" he asked stroking her back.

"Tell me when you are ready honey. Tell me before you do something stupid," she said soothingly.

Gavin remained silent for a long time. He did not talk to Trudy during the drive home. He sat thinking in vain for some way to clear this mess. Nothing struck him and after a while, Gavin succumbed to sleep. Gavin had vivid flashes in his dream, each involving the victims of the death card. Gavin woke up, unable to sleep anymore. As he walked to the dining room, he saw Rebecca standing on a stool, trying to take something from the top shelf.

He saw the stool wobble and instinctively rushed forward. He caught Rebecca as she fell backwards. He looked to the side to see the chair that would have broken her neck had he not interfered.

Noticing that she still wore the same tube top, Gavin growled, "Get changed Becky". Still not having recovered from the shock, Rebecca blinked.

"Get changed. Throw that top away," he repeated once more.

"What?" she asked confused.

"Wear something else," said Gavin except that he was shouting now.

"Gavin, don't be rid......," started Rebecca when Gavin lost his patience. Trudy had come in, having heard the raised voices.

"Forgive me Becky. I have to do this," said Gavin walking towards her with his arms extended.

Perhaps she saw it in his face but Rebecca ran behind Trudy to protect herself. Gavin began to try and grab at her when Trudy screamed, "What the hell are you doing?"

Gavin came back to his senses. "Tell her to change into something else Trudy. It is a matter of life and death," he begged.

"Get out of here," she snarled and Gavin cowered. He walked back to his room and threw himself onto the bed. After about fifteen minutes, there was a knock on the door. Gavin looked to see Rebecca.

"I'm ….," he began apologetically.

"Trudy already did on your behalf," she said and slowly came closer. She had changed her top. "Are you happy now?" she asked pointing to the dress.

"You don't understand …," began Gavin.

"I don't need to Gav. It's hard for all of us given how quickly and how brutally mom and dad were taken away from us," she said soothingly, "I will always be there for you. No matter how many more break-downs you have," she said.

Gavin smiled at her. She knew nothing but he was able to see how ignorance was bliss. Rebecca sat next to him and they began to chat, reminiscing their childhood for what seemed to be hours.

Rebecca smiled that day. It was the first time she did since their mom died. The rest of the day was filled with missed emotions. It was a pleasant week despite the fact that they had their father's funeral.

Rebecca decided to take Nellie out and left to pick her up at the school. Gavin waved goodbye and then noticed something shining on the tire trail. As he stepped forward to have a closer look, his heart began to beat faster. There were not one but two cards. He turned the cards nervously only to see Nellie and Rebecca.

"No," he shouted.

Trudy came out, hearing him. "What happened?" she asked.

"Get your car," he hissed, "We have to go …. NOW"

"What's the matter?" she asked in confusion.

"No time to explain. Let's go," he barked.

Trudy looked bewildered but she did not protest. They were on the road in two minutes. Gavin had taken the wheel and he was driving several miles above the speed limit.

"What's wrong Gav? You've never driven this fast honey. Care to slow down?" she said sounding concerned.

"Bad things are happening," he said.

"What do you mean?" she asked.

"Becky's and Nellie's lives are in danger," he said.

"What? Are you crazy?" asked Trudy.

"I am serious Trudy. Something's happening," began Gavin but stopped as he saw Rebecca and Nellie get into the car, a few hundred feet away. Before he could reach them, Becky drove away into traffic. Gavin tried to get closer but the traffic did not help him.

Then it happened. Just as Becky entered the bridge, a truck swerved sharply, pushing Becky's car off the bridge and into the river, thirty feet below.

Gavin stomped on the brakes and was out of the car and darting towards the bridge in seconds. Wasting no time, Gavin dived into the water. Gavin tried searching underwater in vain. The river was too deep for him to reach the sinking car.

Gavin was helped by a nurse as he sat on a patrol car, covered in a blanket. He did not know how he got there. Trudy stood nearby, holding his hand and tears flowing freely. Neither of them had the situation sink in yet.

It was almost six hours after which the car was pulled out of the water. Gavin noticed a card on the windshield. It was an Ace of Spades. He did not wait to turn the card and look at Trudy's face. He had lost enough. In minutes, he had reached his house. Over the next few hours, Gavin kept running to nearby stores to get supplies after having locked her in his bedroom.

In a matter of hours, he had removed every potentially dangerous object in the bedroom, lined the floor with cushions, covered all the sharp edges. Trudy was genuinely scared but Gavin worked like a maniac.

When Gavin finally got in the room and locked it behind him, Trudy gathered the courage to speak.

"We need to be at the hospital Gavin. We need to ….," she said but choked when she had to say 'collect the bodies'

"We are not going anywhere," said Gavin. He was shivering despite his effort to stay calm.

"They were killed," said Gavin before she could say a word.

"Who were killed?" she asked sounding surprised.

"My mom, Jim, dad and now Becky and Nellie," he said in a whisper.

"Don't be stupid. They were accidents. We were just unlucky," she said.

"Unlucky? One death would have been unlucky. This is something else. You have no idea Trudy," he cried.

"What rubbish is this? Let's go to the hospital Gavin," she said.

"What if I said I knew in advance about these deaths?" he said gravely.

"What do you mean?" she asked.

"There is some curse on me," he said.

"You're scaring me honey," she said coming close to him.

"I'm telling you honey. It all happened at the museum that day," he said gravely.

"What happened?" she asked.

"I brought the wrath of a statue upon myself," he said.

"What wrath? What statue?" asked a puzzled Trudy.

Gavin took a deep breath and began to tell her all that happened. Trudy listened silently and then opened her mouth to say something,

"Don't tell me that it is a coincidence, love," he said sensing what she had in her mind.

"It is weird though," she said.

"I've lost too much already. I won't lose you," he said and hugged her.

Trudy patted his back and kissed his cheek. She did not know whether to believe him or not. However, she knew that Gavin was serious. It had been a strange period for them. Gavin hid the fact that he had seen the card with Trudy's image. It had happened when he sat in the patrol car after his dive into the bridge. He made sure that she stayed within the room. He left the room from time to get anything they wanted. He tested all food on himself before she ate. He knew that she would not be killed before him.

"How long are we going to do this?" asked Trudy after three days.

"As long as it takes," said Gavin.

"Takes to do what? Don't you see that we are our own prisoners?" she asked angrily.

"I can't lose you Trudy. I have to protect you," he said pleadingly.

"How will you protect her?" came a gruff voice from behind him.

Gavin turned to face King Francis who stood casually leaning against the door.

"You?" shouted Gavin in surprise.

Francis just smiled. "Who's that Gavin?" asked Trudy in surprise.

"I'm King Francis the terrible," he said proudly. "I shall now kill you," he said walking towards Trudy.

Gavin blindly charged at him but King Francis vanished in the last second. Gavin stared around frantically, slowly moving towards Trudy. Francis kept appearing in different parts of the room and kept vanishing when Gavin tried to attack him.

In a little while, Gavin found that he was near the door. He grabbed Trudy's hand and made a run for it.

Gavin couldn't see Francis but his voice was heard. "You can't run from me," said the voice cackling loudly.

"Where are we going?" asked Trudy.

"Do you trust me, Trudy?" he asked her.

"Why wouldn't I?" she retorted.

"I need you to come with me. If I can protect you just a little longer, I can save you," he said.

Trudy stopped running. Gavin looked at her questioningly. Before he could speak, she rushed at him and kissed him.

"Is this the time?" he said pushing her.

"Maybe the last time," said Trudy with a weak smile. Her eyes however, had welled up.

"Nobody is taking you from me," said Gavin grabbing her hand.

A knife came hurling at them from the kitchen. Gavin pulled Trudy aside. Within moments, they were in the car.

"Where are we going?" she asked.

"To the place where it all started," he said taking the wheel.

The drive to the museum was most unusual. At one point, Gavin could not help but wonder if it was the normal path or a derby bowl. Unhurt, they reached the museum but their car was in tatters. It was about midnight and all of a sudden, the cars that pursued them disappeared. Gavin did the only thing that struck him. He immediately began to hack into the system.

Within minutes, he was in front of the exhibit of King Francis. Gavin took the axe near the fire hose and approached the statue.

"You did not think it would be that easy, did you?" said King Francis. He had appeared next to Trudy all of a sudden. She attempted to run towards Gavin but Francis caught her hand.

Gavin raised his axe, ready to strike the statue.

"I will kill her," said Francis.

"Not if I finish you first," said Gavin swinging the axe with all his might. The axe struck hard and with an earsplitting sound, separated the head of the statue. Gavin turned to find Trudy standing alone. She was still in shock but his plan had worked. Gavin heaved a sigh of relief as he saw that King Francis had disappeared.

Just as he smiled at Trudy, he felt a sharp pain below his ribs on the left side. He looked forward to see King Francis. His face contorted with fury, the King's eyes were red. He had sunk his fist into Gavin's body. Overwhelmed by pain, Gavin sank to his knees.

"You think you have won, have you?" he said angrily, stressing on every syllable.

Francis then turned to look at Trudy, his hand clenching within Gavin's body. Gavin sank to his knees in pain while saying weakly, "No. Please. Let her go".

"Why should I listen to you? I will not let you die. Not yet," he said reaching in and gripping what felt like Gavin's heart.

"You will not die until you see me bleed your girlfriend to death," he said and began to cackle madly.

As Gavin sat incapacitated, a slit appeared on Trudy's neck. She smiled one last time amidst her tears and slowly sank to the floor. Gavin could see her life drain away in her eyes through his tears.

King Francis took his hand out of Gavin's body and Gavin fell to the floor. He could see Trudy on the floor. Her hand was still twitching slightly. Just as kept watching, the hand stopped twitching. Gavin slowly crawled towards her, with each move giving him searing pain and causing loss of more blood.

When Gavin could no longer move, he rolled over and let go. Tears flowed from his eyes but he was too weak to cry. With much effort, he screamed in agony and anger.

***

Gavin woke in his bed. Trudy was sitting next to him, still working on what looked like their finances. Gavin looked at the date. He had taken Nellie to the museum only hours ago.

"Bad dream?" asked Trudy as she jabbed at her calculator.

"Very bad," he said moving over to lean on her.

The phone rang just as it had done so before, on the exact time.

"What?" he asked.

She raised her hand to stop him. She spoke for a minute and then ended the call with a deep breath.

"What is it?" he asked anxiously hoping that it was not happening again.

"It was your dad," she said.

"And?" he asked.

"He asked me if we could come there for a few days. Your mom wants to spend a few days with her favourite son and his fiancée," she said.

"That's it," he asked in relief.

"What did you expect?" she asked with a smile.

Gavin wasted no time. He swooped to kiss her and started working on her clothes.

"Wait. Are we going?" she asked.

"Not before ….," he said pointedly as he caressed her cheek and passionately kissed her. As he opened his eyes, his head jolted. On the bedside table, he saw a card. It was an Ace of Spades. Gavin reached over nervously to pick up the card that was propped against the lamp on the bedside table.

Trudy overpowered him and they rolled over. She was on top of him and began to kiss him but Gavin was staring at the card. Gavin reached for the card and picked it up. He turned it around nervously.

*****

About the Author

Venkat Raman V

Venkat Raman V is a banker by profession and a writer by passion. He is an internationally published researcher with a fondness for storytelling. Having written for several magazines and publications, he frequently posts on Instagram on his handle *@VVRamanWrites*. He has an anthology series on Kindle called 'Scribbles in the back-benches'.

www.ingramcontent.com/pod-product-compliance
Lightning Source LLC
LaVergne TN
LVHW041639070526
838199LV00052B/3461